arent:
Your child's lov

FR
OF

Every child learns to read in a different way and at his or her own speed. You can help your young reader improve and become more confident by encouraging his or her own interests and abilities. You can also guide your child's spiritual development by reading stories with biblical values and Bible stories, like I Can Read! books published by Zonderkidz. From books your child reads with you to the first books he or she reads alone, there are I Can Read! books for every stage of reading:

My First — SHARED READING
Basic language, word repetition, and whimsical illustrations, ideal for sharing with your emergent reader.

1 — BEGINNING READING
Short sentences, familiar words, and simple concepts for children eager to read on their own.

2 — READING WITH HELP
Engaging stories, longer sentences, and language play for developing readers.

3 — READING ALONE
Complex plots, challenging vocabulary, and high-interest topics for the independent reader.

4 — ADVANCED READING
Short paragraphs, chapters, and exciting themes for the perfect bridge to chapter books.

I Can Read! books have introduced children to the joy of reading since 1957. Featuring award-winning authors and illustrators and a fabulous cast of beloved characters, I Can Read! books set the standard for beginning readers.

Lexile: _____

AR/BL: _____

AR Points: _____

magical words **"I Can Read!"**

nriching your child's reading experience.
Zonderkidz I Can Read! titles.

You have made the heavens and the earth
by your great power and outstretched arm.
Nothing is too hard for you.
—*Jeremiah 32:17*

Otter and Owl Set Sail
Copyright © 2008 by Crystal Bowman
Illustrations copyright © 2008 by Kevin Zimmer

Requests for information should be addressed to:
Zonderkidz, Grand Rapids, Michigan 49530

Library of Congress Cataloging-in-Publication Data:

Bowman, Crystal.
  Otter and Owl set sail / written by Crystal Bowman ; illustrated by Kevin Zimmer.
    p. cm.
  ISBN 978-0-310-71704-1 (softcpver : alk. paper) [1. Otters–Fiction. 2. Owls–Fiction. 3. Sailing–
Fiction. 4. Christian life–Fiction.] I. Zimmer, Kevin, ill. II. Title.
  PZ7.B6834Oy 2008
  [E–dc22

                                                                                      2008009586

Zonderkidz is a trademark of Zondervan.

Art Direction and Design: Jody Langley

Printed in China

08 09 10 • 4 3 2 1

Otter and Owl
Set Sail

story by Crystal Bowman

pictures by Kevin Zimmer

Owl sat on a stump by the pond.

He heard a noise in the bushes.

It was his friend Otter.

"Boo!" said Otter. "Did I scare you?"

"No," said Owl.

"I am too busy thinking."

"I am thinking about

making a sailboat," said Owl.

"How will you do that?" asked Otter.

"Well," said Owl.

"We already have a raft.

All we need is a sail."

Otter saw an old shirt by the bush.

"How about this?" asked Otter.

"That will do," said Owl.

Owl put the sail on a big stick.

Then he tied the ends of the sail

to the front and back of the raft.

"Our sailboat is ready to sail,"

said Owl.

"Let's go for a ride," said Otter.

Otter and Owl got in the boat.

Otter bounced up and down.

"Here we go!" said Otter.

They waited and waited.

But the sailboat did not sail.

"I will have to think," said Owl.

Owl thought and thought.

Then he had an idea.

"Let's blow on the sail," said Owl.

Otter and Owl blew and blew.

"Blow harder!" said Owl.

Otter and Owl blew harder.

They blew and blew

until their faces were purple.

But the sailboat did not sail.

"I will think some more," said Owl.

Owl thought and thought.

But he didn't know what to do.

"I know!" said Otter.

"Let's sing a sailing song."

Otter and Owl began to sing.

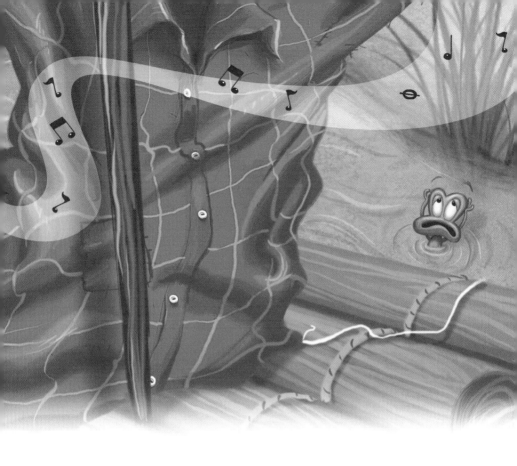

"Sailing, sailing,

over the big blue pond."

"Sing louder," said Otter.

Otter and Owl sang louder and louder.

They sang the song over and over.

But the sailboat did not sail.

Owl thought and thought some more.

"I have one more idea," he said.

"Let's turn the sail around."

Otter and Owl tried to turn

the sail around.

Splash!

They both fell into the water.

Otter and Owl got back into the boat.

"Let's try it again," said Owl.

They turned the sail around.

Otter bounced up and down.

"Here we go!" said Otter.

Otter and Owl waited and waited.

But the sailboat did not sail.

Owl was sad.

"I made a bad sailboat," he said.

"Our sailboat will never sail."

"You made a fine sailboat.

All we need is wind," said Otter.

"I cannot make wind," said Owl.

"No," said Otter. "But God can.

God makes clouds and rain and snow.

And he makes wind."

Owl looked at the trees.

The leaves were not blowing.

"God did not make wind today,"

Owl said.

"Let's go home."

Owl went to his house.

Otter went to his house next door.

Owl ate noodle soup

for dinner.

Otter ate pizza.

Then they both went to bed.

The next morning,

Owl looked out the window.

He saw the leaves blowing.

He ran to Otter's house.

"Wake up, Otter," he said.

"God made wind today!"

Otter and Owl ran to the pond.

They climbed on the raft.

They did not blow the sail.

They did not sing a sailing song.

They did not turn the sail around.

"Here we go!" said Otter.

"Here we go!" said Owl.

The wind blew the sail.

The raft began to move.

Otter and Owl sailed all the way
to the other side of the pond.